BARON OF BROWN STREET

by Eric Mansfield

BARON OF BROWN STREET

SPECIAL NOTE

Anyone receiving permission to produce BARON OF BROWN STREET is required to give credit to the Author as sole and exclusive Author of the Play on the title page of all programs distributed in connection with performances of the Play and in all instances in which the title of the Play appears for purposes of advertising, publicizing or otherwise exploiting the Play and/or a production thereof. The name of the Author must appear on a separate line, in which no other name appears, immediately beneath the title and in size of type equal to 50% of the size of the largest, most prominent letter used for the title of the Play. No person, firm, or entity may receive credit larger or more prominent than that accorded the Author.

SPECIAL NOTE ON SONGS AND RECORDINGS

For performances of copyrighted songs, arrangements or recordings mentioned in these Plays, the permission of the copyright owner(s) must be obtained. Other songs, arrangements or recordings may be substituted provided permission from the copyright owner(s) of such songs, arrangements or recordings is obtained; or songs, arrangements or recordings in the public domain may be substituted.

Book Cover: Cennidie Hall
Book Design: Jonathan Cook
First Edition: June 2024
ISBN 978-1-964045-04-7

- For Lenny King, wherever you are. Please know the impact a single meaningful conversation can have on a world quick to judge you and others who have survived the worst the world can throw their way.

BARON OF BROWN STREET, which is inspired by the true story of Lenny King, received the 2023 Jean Kennedy Smith National Playwrighting Award (2nd Place) from the Kennedy Center in Washington, D.C.

The play by Eric Mansfield had its professional (AEA) world premiere at Rubber City Theatre in Akron, OH in September 2023. The production was directed by Joe Soriano and the cast was as follows:

LENNY . . . . Brian O. Jackson (AEA)
BOB, MARK, PUNK2 . . . . David Bays
COLLIN, JONATHON, PUNK 1 . . . . Zach Palumbo
JAMIE, NICKIE, MARY, RITA . . . . Isabelle Bailey
ERICA, DEANNA, ALLY . . . . Cait McNeal
TYLER, ELON . . . . Andrew Keller

SCENIC/LIGHTING DESIGNER . . . . . . Dane CT Leasure
COSTUME DESIGNER . . . . Irene Mack-Shafer
INTIMACY DIRECTOR . . . . Julia Fisher
STAGE MANAGER . . . . Barbara Kozlov
MARKETING/SOCIAL MEDIA . . . . Cennidie Hall
HEAD OF WARDROBE . . . . Kendra Strickland

BARON OF BROWN STREET

CHARACTERS

LENNY
45-55, homeless man who has recently returned to living under the Brown Street Bridge after being hospitalized when he was attacked by some street punks. He likes and generally cares about people, but right now just wants some peace and quiet following the attack.

******Note****: With doubling, a minimum of five actors (3M, 2F) can play the 15 parts below that come in and out of Lenny's world. The producing theatre may cast the roles however they see fit. Gender/Race of all characters, unless noted, may be modified to meet cast needs.*

BOB
local newspaper editor.

COLLIN
uppity attorney.

JAMIE
college student studying photography.

MARK
homeless man, who was also attacked the night Lenny was burned.

ERICA & NICKIE
paramedics who look out for Lenny's well-being.

PUNK 1 & PUNK 2
they're street punks up to no good.

JONATHAN
minister of local community church.

MARY
pushy church leader with Jonathan.

DEANNA
Inquisitive sociology doctor

TYLER
Lenny's son, 24, who hasn't seen his dad since he was 12.

ELON & RITA
arrogant banker and his pompous PR mouthpiece.

ALLY
Lenny's former high school student who is now grown and has her own family living in Ohio.

TIME & PLACE
The play is divided into 16 linear scenes that take place under a bridge over a five-day period.

AUTHOR NOTES

Scenes are meant to flow continuously unless otherwise noted, although the time between scenes can vary. As the entire play takes place under a bridge, hearing cars driving by above on Brown Street would be appropriate. Lenny's hearing is fading, so he should often lean in to hear those speaking to him or even intimate that they speak louder or repeat themselves.

The actor playing Lenny must play (or quickly learn) a few basic chords on the acoustic guitar. While the script calls for Lenny to play and sing the opening lines of "Dust in the Wind" by Kansas, the playwright has not secured the rights to this music. Productions may choose instead to have Lenny play a few emotional chords of his choosing and then deliver a single spoken line of "All we are is dust in the wind."

/   Indicates that the next line of dialogue should overlap.
...   Indicates non-verbal response
(beat)   Indicates an intentional pause for effect lasting at least as long as it would take to say the word "beat."

SCENE 1

A camping tent is erected under the old Brown Street Bridge near McKinley Avenue in South Central Akron, Ohio. There are bushes, some grass, trash and a burned-out mattress nearby. Several five-gallon buckets are visible as make-shift stools along with an old camping/folding chair, and a fire bucket/ring/pit. The walls under the bridge sport graffiti, which includes some musical notes Lenny probably put there himself, including the phrase "the world showed no compassion to me." There are leaves, sticks and general wildlife that would grow around the bottom of a city bridge. The paths in and out of the site make it clear someone has made this space their living area for some time.

Sunrise on Sunday morning as cars can be heard traveling over the bridge combined with the morning yawns of birds and wildlife. The tent looks empty as Bob, a local newspaper reporter, enters carrying multiple copies of that day's morning paper As this is the second time Bob has visited Lenny's campsite, Bob's approach should feel familiar but not completely comfortable.

BOB: Lenny? Lenny you in there? It's uh . . . Bob Simons from the Gazette. We spoke last week.

(Bob checks in the tent, but no one is home. Just as he is about to give up and leave, Lenny sits up in the bushes where he'd been sleeping next to his tent. His long unkempt hair falls down over the left side of his face, so

we're only seeing one of Lenny's eyes.)

LENNY: Whatchoo want?

BOB: Lenny? Oh. Lenny. It's . . . Bob Simons.

LENNY: Who? Who'd you say you are?

BOB: Bob Simons. We spoke five days ago. Why aren't you sleeping in your tent?

(Lenny stands and walks past Bob to the tent, crawling in face first with his butt crack visible to the audience.)

LENNY: Sleep where I want to.

BOB: *(speaking into the tent's side mesh windows)* I brought you copies of your story. Like I told you I would.

LENNY: Yep.

BOB: There's a color photo of you on the front page. And… with today being Sunday . . . it's the most read day of the week. Lots of people are reading your story, Lenny.

(Lenny spins around so he is sitting in the tent's door looking out at Bob. Lenny uses a hairbrush to whip his dirty locks back and finally puts on a baseball hat. He intentionally keeps his hair down on the left side of his face as though he is hiding it from view.)

LENNY: Uh-huh. Figured you were coming.

BOB: I uh . . . brought you five copies. *(hands him the newspapers)* Courtesy of the Gazette. You want to read it?

LENNY: Don't need to.

BOB: Oh . . . can you not? Um . . . or do you want me to just read it to / you?

LENNY: I can read Bob. Not ignorant.

BOB: Think you mean illiter-- ya know, here.

(Bob rotates the paper in Lenny's hands. Lenny begins scanning the copy. After only a few seconds, he stops and puts the extra four copies in his tent.)

LENNY: Yep.

BOB: You're . . . you're done? How fast do you read?

LENNY: Told you I didn't need to read / it.

BOB: Don't you want to know what it says?

LENNY: I know what it says.

BOB: You might think you do based on our / interview.

LENNY: People been coming down since Friday with printouts of your epic story. Wanting to show it to me and read it to me.

BOB: Oh.

LENNY: Yeah?

BOB: Ah, I get it. The story was posted Friday on our website. But it's the physical paper that's worth saving, and that's what I brought you.

(Lenny holds up the headline "King of Brown Street.")

LENNY: Your idea?

BOB: It's a play on words. Your name is Lenny King. This here . . . this area . . . your tent . . . it's your castle. Right here under Brown Street.

LENNY: Uh huh.

BOB: King. Castle. Just storytelling. With a name like King, it felt right to create that moniker for / you.

LENNY: I ain't no king. *(beat)* I ain't no king.

BOB: I can have it removed online, but --

LENNY: Speak up.

BOB: I was saying I can have it changed on the internet… but if you just look at the headline and how the story / is told.

LENNY: You deaf?

(As Bob continues speaking, Lenny retains the front page with its big headline and tosses the rest of the edition inside his tent. Lenny takes a bottle of water and positions himself behind the tent for partial privacy as he washes his hands, uses the fresh newspaper to dry them, and then uses the moist newspaper in a sort of a morning sponge bath.)

BOB: I put a lot of thought into telling your story . . . and you do have an amazing, incredible journey, Lenny. You really do.

LENNY: Yep.

BOB: I wanted it to be authentic and to let you tell your story. You'll recall I recorded our conversations . . . so that I'd have your exact words about being attacked. And the horror you endured being set on . . . by . . . by being doused with lighter fluid . . . and then set on fire.

LENNY: Uh huh.

BOB: And already we're getting calls from people wanting to step up and help you.

LENNY: *(washing behind the tent)* Don't want it. Don't need it.

BOB: People are inspired by your journey, and that doesn't

happen every day.

LENNY: What doesn't?

BOB: Inspiration. Sometimes we print incredible stories and hear crickets. But your experience has our phones jumping off the hook. And on a Sunday morning.

LENNY: I know what day it is.

BOB: The readers can feel your pain / Lenny.

LENNY: Can they now?

BOB: So they aren't just interested in how you ended up homeless with nothing.

LENNY: Who said I had nothing?

BOB: *(stumbling for the right words)* Well . . . because you're, ya know, homeless, Lenny.

LENNY: Mmm mmm.

BOB: But not just that. They're really moved by your heart.

(Lenny is finished bathing. He returns to the front of the tent as Bob continues to talk.)

Forgiving those punks for what they did to you and to Mark. That just doesn't happen every day.

LENNY: What doesn't?

BOB: Forgiveness.

LENNY: Why?

BOB: Why what?

LENNY: Why doesn't forgiveness happen every day?

BOB: That's the point. It's unique what you've / done.

LENNY: Shouldn't that be your story?

BOB: . . .

LENNY: Shouldn't that be your headline? Why people can't

fogive ch'other? Stead of writing about a guy ain't none of em ever heard of?

BOB: I think that'd be a great sidebar for my editor.

LENNY: Side what?

BOB: Lenny. Seriously. I just want to thank you for being so candid and trusting me with your story. I can't tell you how much that means to me.

LENNY: . . .

BOB: With your permission, I'd like to let this story simmer til the end of the week . . . and then come back and do a follow-up.

LENNY: Another story? Bout me?

BOB: Yeah, of what it's been like for you. You just said people have read this story. And they're telling you how inspiring you are. And thanking you for setting an example.

LENNY: Never said anyone thanked me. Said they came down here.

BOB: Maybe one of them . . . will also have a kind heart -- just like you -- and they can take you in.

LENNY: That why you did your story?

BOB: I'm sorry?

LENNY: That why you wrote it? So someone who read about ol' Lenny under the bridge can come gawk at me? Trespass on my home?

BOB: We wanted a good result, yes.

LENNY: Uh-huh.

BOB: Shows how we as journalists can make life better / for others.

LENNY: So you did this fo me? To make my life better?

BOB: Lenny, what do you want from me?

LENNY: Nothin. You came to me with this, remember?

BOB: I just wanted you to know . . . I'd like another interview. And I wanted to give you copies so you could share.

LENNY: With who?

BOB: With . . . uh . . . anyone you like. Look, I'll be back Friday morning . . . and then we can chat for the follow-up / story.

(Bob starts to leave.)

LENNY: Bringing me a Big Mac again?

BOB: Do you want me to bring you McDonalds?

LENNY: Just saying . . . you did last time. But not this time.

BOB: Well, I'd be glad to bring you McDonald's, Lenny.

LENNY: Just saying when you wanted something from me, you brought me a Big Mac. And when you didn't, you didn't.

BOB: *(leaving)* You'll have a full moon this week, and it looks like the snow might arrive soon, so stay warm. See ya Friday, Lenny.

(Bob exits.)

SCENE 2

Lenny crawls into his tent and returns with a small apple and a pocketknife. He sits on a bucket and starts to cut slices when a voice comes from above.

COLLIN: *(offstage)* Hello? Anyone down there?

(Lenny ignores the voice and continues to eat.)

Mr. King? Hello?

(Collin, a well-dressed, uppity attorney appears out of breath from crawling down the hill next to the bridge to reach the tent.)

There you are. Wow. It's quite a hike to get to / you.

LENNY: There's a path around over there.

COLLIN: Excuse me?

LENNY: Path over there. Didn't have to come down the hill.

COLLIN: I'll remember that. Collin Lockworth. Here's my card. Nice to meet you, Mr. King.

LENNY: Lenny.

COLLIN: Lenny.

LENNY: Yep.

COLLIN: Thought you were going to say: "Mr. King? You must be looking for my father." *(laughs alone)*

LENNY: Why's that?

COLLIN: Just a common joke men like me . . . / say.

LENNY: Whachoo want?

COLLIN: Mind if I sit?

(Lenny gestures Collin to turn over another bucket and sit with him. He does so, using a handkerchief to wipe off the bucket before sitting on it.)

Wow. This is, ah, more comfortable than it looks.

LENNY: Really?

COLLIN: Mr. King, let me cut right to the point. I saw your story in the Gazette.

LENNY: No kidding.

COLLIN: And then I looked up your case on-line. I hope that was ok. And I, uh, really think you are missing out on the compensation you're rightfully / owed.

LENNY: Compensation?

COLLIN: Yes. Absolutely.

LENNY: Those boys went to jail didn't they?

COLLIN: Not just boys. They were all convicted as adults, so they're men.

LENNY: They're boys. Trust me, ain't a one of them a man.

COLLIN: Well they owe you.

LENNY: Owe me what?

COLLIN: Mr. King, what they did to you and to Mr. Thompson . . . I don't think you understand the value of your injuries.

LENNY: Value? You think them nights in the burn unit was valuable?

COLLIN: In a civil court, you win.

LENNY: Win what?

COLLIN: Financial payments for your injuries.

LENNY: Money?

COLLIN: Well, yes.

LENNY: Don't want it. Don't need it.

COLLIN: You're entitled.

LENNY: From dem boys? They ain't got no money.

COLLIN: That's the thing. Their parents do?

LENNY: What their parents got to do with this?

COLLIN: Everything. Mom and dad should have known what their kids were really doing. My God, they beat you and set you on fire. They're responsible.

LENNY: No they ain't.

COLLIN: Legally, they are.

LENNY: I ain't never met em. They ain't caused me no grief.

COLLIN: That's the thing. You don't have to have met their moms and dads for them to be held responsible in court.

LENNY: Now they have to be judged too? For being a parent?

COLLIN: For being a bad parent. Yeah.

LENNY: And who decides who is a bad parent? Just cuz their kids went to jail?

COLLIN: Kids do bad things when parents aren't around.

LENNY: Uh huh.

COLLIN: They do. You'd know this if you were a parent.

(Lenny shoots Collin a look.)

Look. I can get this settlement for you. All you'd have to do is sign a few / documents.

LENNY: Why I want to take their money?

COLLIN: *(talking down to Lenny)* So you can have a better life and get the hell out of this shithole you call a home.

LENNY: *(gesturing slightly with his knife)* Think it's time you left.

COLLIN: I didn't mean to offend. You have my card there.

LENNY: Goodbye. Git.

COLLIN: You could call me or . . . well, you don't have a

phone, do you? I'll stop back Friday morning. See if you've changed your mind because I know I can get you maybe as much as a million dollars.

LENNY: A million dollars?

COLLIN: Can you imagine?

LENNY: Don't want it. Don't need it. Path's over there.

COLLIN: Thank you for your time, Mr. King.

(Collin begins to leave.)

LENNY: How much you get?

COLLIN: Excuse me?

LENNY: How much you get? Something like this. What's your rake?

COLLIN: Just standard legal fees.

LENNY: I'm a standard man.

COLLIN: A third. One third of the settlement. But with what you'd be awarded, you'd be so much better off / Mr. King.

LENNY: Path's over there. *(beat)* Ain't gonna ask you again.

(Collin realizes the conversation is over. He brushes himself off like he's been crawling in filth and then departs. Lenny chews a bit more on his apple and sits deep in thought.)

SCENE 3

Lenny pauses thinking he heard something. He's about to take a bite when he pauses again, this time hearing a camera clicking. Startled, he stands up and hears more camera clicks.

LENNY: Who's there? I hear you. Come out here. Show yourself.

(Jamie, a creative college student, appears from under the bridge.)

JAMIE: Um. So sorry. Hello there Mr. King.

LENNY: Let me see you. Step out here. Now.

(Jamie steps fully into view.)

JAMIE: Just got a camera here. No weapon. Noooo threat to you. No harm intended.

LENNY: Whachoo want?

JAMIE: I'm here to take your . . . well, let me start over. Hi. I'm Jamie Eastman. A sophomore studying photography.

LENNY: No shit.

JAMIE: And I've been assigned to do a photo essay for my urban life class . . . and I thought . . . after reading about you . . .

(She unfolds a copy of the newspaper headline.)

Have you seen this article? You're on the front page.

LENNY: . . .

JAMIE: I thought you would be a phenomenal photo story. Of you and how you're living . . . and ya know, showing people what you go through every day.

LENNY: What I go through?

JAMIE: Ya know, much much deeper than, ya know . . . than the Gazette was able to show here in the article.

LENNY: Why don't you feature the Landons?

JAMIE: The Landons? I'm sorry. I'm not familiar with what you're talking / about.

LENNY: Not what. Who.

JAMIE: Who you're talking about.

LENNY: The family three blocks over? Lost everything in a fire a few weeks ago? When I was at the courthouse, I read about them in the paper.

JAMIE: Yeah but I want to / feature you.

LENNY: Just yesterday, I stopped over to First National to donate a few bucks to their fund. It was in their story. And the bank wouldn't take my money.

JAMIE: I don't understand.

LENNY: Their fund had been closed because no one . . . no one in this town . . . had donated a nickel. So they closed it. A whole family right here in Akron and featured in the paper same as me . . . and no one gave a cent to them.

JAMIE: Seems a bit odd.

LENNY: The bank told me I could still donate if I wanted to.

JAMIE: Did you?

LENNY: Said they had a fund to help the people in India from a Tsunami. Said folks contribute to that one every day. But for the Landons . . . *(look of disbelief)*

JAMIE: Sooooo . . . would it be ok . . . if I take some photos for my / assignment?

LENNY: Without my permission?

JAMIE: Technically, ya know . . . legally you're in the public view so I don't . . . have . . . to . . .

(Lenny shoots Jamie a look of defiance.)

Ya know, you're right. Um, Mr. King. May I have permission to photograph you? Nothing bad. Nothing bad at all. Just what it's like for you, ya know, here. Under the Brown Street bridge.

LENNY: You see a sign that reads "zoo" anywhere?

JAMIE: Um, no.

LENNY: Then why you treating me like an animal?

JAMIE: I didn't mean to upset you.

LENNY: I ain't no elephant. I ain't no tiger. I ain't no giraffe.

(He snatches Jamie's newspaper.)

And I ain't no king either.

(He crumples the paper.)

JAMIE: I'm really, really sorry. I didn't mean to upset you, Mr. King.

LENNY: Lenny.

JAMIE: I didn't mean to hurt your feelings . . . um . . . Lenny.

LENNY: What you really come to see?

JAMIE: I, ah, told you. I came to see you. And to photograph you . . . and where you / live.

LENNY: No, you didn't.

JAMIE: I told you. I attend the university, and I have an assignment / for class.

LENNY: But that's not what you came for. Is it?

JAMIE: . . .

LENNY: You want to see if old burned-up Lenny looks like Phantom of the Opera don't you?

JAMIE: No. No. Nooooo, that's not why I came down here.

LENNY: You want to see my scars?

JAMIE: Noooo. Unless you want to show me . . . uh . . . ya know . . . that's not what I'm asking for. I'm sorry if it seemed / like it.

LENNY: You think showing everyone what a burned-up vagabond really looks like will win you some kinda photo award?

JAMIE: Noooooooo. I just wanted to meet you and take your picture. And I can, ya know, be gone in a few minutes.

LENNY: A few minutes?

JAMIE: Yeah.

LENNY: Gone? You'll leave me alone?

JAMIE: I could come back with copies of the photos if you / like.

LENNY: Don't want em. Don't need em.

JAMIE: Ok . . .

(Lenny sits down on his bucket in front of his tent.)

LENNY: Fine. Take your damn photos.

(Jamie begins snapping photos from different angles. She stops when she trips on the burned-out mattress.)

JAMIE: You have a mattress outside your tent?

LENNY: Not mine.

JAMIE: Whose is it?

LENNY: Anyone who needs a place for the night.

JAMIE: So, anyone?

LENNY: Not everyone's as well off as I am. *(beat)* No one should have to sleep on the ground.

JAMIE: Does it get used?

LENNY: Mark used it.

JAMIE: Oh. Um, ok.

(After a few more shots, Lenny stands proudly as Jamie continues to shoot photos.)

LENNY: Got enough?

JAMIE: Just need one more . . . a character shot as they call them.

LENNY: A what?

JAMIE: Character shot.

LENNY: Character?

JAMIE: Something with, ya know, your personality.

(Jamie raises her camera to her eye. With his back to the audience, Lenny walks directly to Jamie's camera and stops just a few feet away. He pulls back his hair to reveal his entire face to Jamie, who pauses and then lowers her camera without taking a photo.)

I . . . appreciate your allowing me to . . . uh . . . goodbye, Mr. King. Um, Lenny. Bye.

(Jamie exits under the bridge and out of sight. Lenny watches her go and then turns around so that the

audience sees his face fully for the first time and recognizes that his face is not burned. He ties his hair in a ponytail.)

SCENE 4

Mark approaches wearing an old blue jean jacket. He has a bruise on his cheek and what looks like blood stains on his jeans.

MARK: New girlfriend?

LENNY: . . .

MARK: Love the Phantom reference.

LENNY: Stop.

MARK: Always said you'd have been great getting out of the pit and into the musical ya / know.

LENNY: *(chuckles)* Especially the end where the Phantom magically disappears.

MARK: Touché.

LENNY: She asked about your bed, smartass.

MARK: She can have it. Didn't bring me any luck. What's with all the foot traffic down here anyway?

(Lenny reaches into the tent and hands Mark a copy of the paper.)

(majestic) King of Brown Street.

LENNY: Don't start.

MARK: Well apparently you're royalty now. *(mocking a*

bow) A pleasure it is to serve the throne.

LENNY: Mark.

MARK: What? You did a good thing. Good to see you recognized for it.

LENNY: I ain't no king.

MARK: Fine be a Lord, or a Count, or . . . how about a Baron? It's still nobility, but Barons work for a living.

LENNY: A Baron?

MARK: Why not?

LENNY: Fine, but for all this journalistic notoriety, my arms are just begging for some relief.

MARK: Begging kind of goes with the whole "living-under-a-bridge" motif.

LENNY: I guess.

MARK: You eat today? Really eat? Besides that old apple?

LENNY: . . .

MARK: Leftover, rotten fruit from the Brown Street Market is ok . . . but don't be some stubborn ass of a man. Shelter has good soup on / Sundays.

LENNY: The shelter? Remember what happened last time we were / there?

MARK: No. Remind me again about getting our shoes and jackets taken by those losers.

LENNY: I meant seeing . . . you know.

MARK: Oh. You know he's gonna find you again.

(Mark stretches out on the burned-out mattress.)

LENNY: He'll look. He always looks.

MARK: Well, being in the newspaper means he now knows where to look.

LENNY: Kid doesn't need me in his life.

MARK: Why you gotta be like that?

LENNY: Like what?

MARK: *(sitting up on the mattress)* Like you're all glad-to-love-and-forgive everyone else. Even those flame-throwing street freaks. But God forbid you forgive yourself.

LENNY: Stop --

MARK: Or let your son forgive / you.

LENNY: Yeah, well . . . shit.

MARK: You know I'm right.

LENNY: C'mon man. I at least need you to be on my side / today.

MARK: I am on your side. Which side is your good side again?

LENNY: Whichever side isn't on fire.

MARK: Haaaa . . . see? There you go. First step towards healing is learning to laugh a little bit.

LENNY: I'm trying.

MARK: Well, try to get a log going will ya. Suns going down, and I don't think the snow's gonna hold off much longer.

LENNY: What? You a weatherman now?

MARK: Oh, and keep your eyes open around here brother. Unless your majesty's gonna dig a moat around this castle . . . you're still out in the open.

LENNY: I'm fine.

MARK: Might want to get yourself some protection. Might need to think about a peace.

(Lenny ignores the idea. He lights a long match and

then stares at it intently as though the flame could speak with memories of why it was used to torture him. He begins to start the fire.)

LENNY: You want to pull the mattress over here to stay warm?

(Lenny looks over his shoulder, but the mattress is empty as Mark is walking away.)

SCENE 5

Two flashlight beams appear under the bridge, but Lenny doesn't react and keeps looking at the fire. Nickie and Erica, two paramedics, appear with a medical bag.

NICKIE: Hey there handsome.

ERICA: Aren't ya gonna welcome us from the darkness? It's me. The ghost of Christmas past.

NICKIE: Thought I was Christmas past?

ERICA: No, you were gonna be Casper.

LENNY: I know your flashlights.

ERICA: Well, we light up your life. See what I did there?

NICKIE: *(to Erica)* You're hopeless.

LENNY: Hi Nickie. Hi Erica.

(Lenny tends to the fire as Nickie and Erica sit down on either side of him.)

ERICA: Why aren't you at the shelter? Lenny, we talked

about this.

LENNY: Ahhhhhh . . . c'mon.

ERICA: We had a deal.

LENNY: Old habits.

NICKIE: Open your jacket. Actually, just go ahead and take it off.

LENNY: Really?

NICKIE: Yessss. Really. You know us. Need to get our thrills any way that we can.

LENNY: Fine.

(With the paramedics' help, Lenny takes off his jacket and his heavy shirt down to just his t-shirt. He has bandages covering the burns on both forearms.)

Had a mom. Don't need two more.

NICKIE: Think of us as the sisters you never wanted.

ERICA: And hey, don't mock being a parent. It's pretty rewarding. Ok. Deep breaths.

(Erica places a stethoscope on Lenny's chest, over his t-shirt. Ad-libs interaction listening to his heart both front and back.)

Good. And again.

(Lenny breathes.)

Good. Sounding real good, Lenny.

NICKIE: My turn. Breathe normal.

(Nickie gently puts a blood pressure sleeve over Lenny's bandaged arm. Ad-libs taking his blood pressure.)

LENNY: Ouch.

NICKIE: Sorry . . . trying to be gentle . . . but you know this has to be snug.

LENNY: Damn.

NICKIE: 122 over 80. Not bad. Glad you're not a smoker. Ok . . . let me see your baby blues.

(Nickie uses a pen flashlight and examines Lenny's pupils.)

Good. Now open wide.

(Lenny sticks out his tongue, and she looks in his mouth.)

LENNY: *(flirting smile)* You get that close, you should kiss me.

NICKIE: Get some mouthwash lover, and then we can talk. *(winks)*

ERICA: Ok . . . now the fun part.

LENNY: We have to?

ERICA: Yes, we have to.

(Erica and Nickie remove the bandages from Lenny's forearms. Ad-libbing chatter/concern/jokes as they use wipes to clean the wounds as Lenny winces. This engagement should feel as though it has happened

several times in recent weeks.)

LENNY: Ahh . . . hate that. God.

(Lenny takes deep breaths while they work on his arms.)

NICKIE: Beats getting an infection. Almost done.

ERICA: And hey, you're getting a 2-for-1 tonight. A lot of patients would pay extra for this.

(Erica and Nickie finish putting fresh bandages on Lenny's arms. He pulls his heavy shirt back over his t-shirt. Nickie hands Lenny fresh bandages.)

NICKIE: Use these in case one comes off.

LENNY: Yeah. Yeah.

NICKIE: Tell me you got it?

LENNY: Got it. Whatever. Ain't you girls got somewhere to be?

ERICA: What could be better than visiting our celebrity patient?

LENNY: Ohhh . . . not you too.

NICKIE: Hey. Neither of us broads have ever been in the paper.

ERICA: It's cool Lenny. We won't ask you to take any selfies. Here.

(Erica hands Lenny a Ziplock bag with a sandwich.)

LENNY: No mayo right?

(Erica nods.)

God I needed this tonight.

ERICA: Right . . . you can eat after one more thing. Close your eyes. You know the drill.

(Lenny closes his eyes. Erica uses her smart phone to make tones to test Lenny's hearing.)

LENNY: *(hears sound on his left side)* F-sharp. *(hears sound on his right side)* B-flat.

ERICA: Alright. You're in tune, but your hearing's still pretty weak. Need to get a specialist to check that out.

NICKIE: Ok. Here's the deal. We know you don't want to leave your tent, so we'll pretend we didn't see you down here. And you can stay on one condition.

LENNY: What's that?

NICKIE: Friday morning . . . you come to the clinic for a more thorough / follow-up.

LENNY: Ohhh . . . man.

NICKIE: That's the deal.

(Nickie and Erica stand up to leave.)

LENNY: I have to?

NICKIE: We're volunteering Friday. We'll get you in and out without any paperwork.

LENNY: But --

NICKIE: No one will see you. We know you don't like the attention. We could also get you a real bed for the night. Would be nice for you.

ERICA: Don't make us come down here and throw you in
the squad. You know we'll do it.

LENNY: . . .

ERICA: Hey, you know I'm just busting your balls, right?

LENNY: *(getting emotional)* I don't know what I would have
done without you / two.

ERICA: Lenny. You don't have to keep saying that. We're
glad we were on call that night . . . for you . . . and for
Mark.

NICKIE: And we were glad to keep checking on you in the
burn unit. But listen to me. *(kneeling and leaning in)*
You listening? The best way to thank us is by taking
care of yourself . . . and making a plan to get out from
under this bridge. Got it?

(Nickie kisses Lenny on the forehead.
He nods yes.)

ERICA: Night, maestro. Be there Friday.

(Lenny blows them a small kiss, and his face says thank
you. Erica and Nickie use their flashlights and head out
the way they came. Lenny opens the sandwich and starts
devouring it next to the fire.)

SCENE 6

Flashlights approach again, but this time with the sound of
loud male voices laughing and cackling. Lenny reacts
quickly and ducks behind his tent to hide. Two punks arrive

and invade the campsite.

PUNK 1: Lenny. Oh Lenny. Where for art thou Lenny?

PUNK 2: What? You Mark Twain now?

PUNK 1: That's not Mark Twain you idiot. That's like Tolstoy or Plato or somebody.

PUNK 2: Shut up. You scared him off. Nice job. Knew you were too loud.

PUNK 1: Fire's still going. Must be in the woods taking a shit or something. *(loudly)* Hope you're having a good shit, Lenny.

PUNK 2: Can't run forever. Couldn't keep your mouth shut could you?

PUNK 1: Like Mark did.

(They both laugh.)

PUNK 2: Should have just stayed quiet and healed. *(loudly)* You hear me King of Brown Street? *(laughs)*

PUNK 1: Next time then. Let's go.

(Punk 2 sees Lenny's half-eaten sandwich.)

PUNK 2: Looks like someone forgot the best part of Thanksgiving.

(He rips up what's left of Lenny's food and tosses it in the woods.)

Gobble Gobble Gobble!

PUNK 1: Hope you can forgive me.

(They laugh and exit.
Lenny stays quiet and hidden until they are gone.)

LENNY: *(from his hiding spot)* Now let it be war upon you both.

SCENE 7

Birds chirping as the sun comes up. Lenny crawls out from behind his tent having had a bad night hiding and sleeping on the ground. He opens a bottle of water and looks towards the sunrise until something catches his eyes in the woods causing him to smile.

Jonathan and Mary, two leaders of a local church, approach on the path. Jonathan is carrying a bible.

JONATHAN: Well top of the morning to you / Mr. King.
LENNY: Shhhhhh.

(Lenny motions them to be quiet. He pulls them in close and points to the woods.)

MARY: *(whispering)* Wow.

(Lenny nods.)

JONATHAN: *(whispering)* They're so little.

(All three watch for a few more seconds before a sound

indicates the baby deer have run off.)

MARY: I can't remember the last time I saw baby deer.

JONATHAN: Gift from God for sure.

LENNY: They say hello to me every morning.

JONATHAN: I think the Lord was trying to say good morning, Lenny. *(laughs)* Guess I will too. Good morning, Lenny.

MARY: Yes. Good morning, Mr. King.

LENNY: Morning.

(Lenny takes off his heavy jacket and pulls on a different, lighter jacket or sweatshirt for the day.)

JONATHAN: You remember us? I'm Jonathan, pastor of the Brown Street church.

MARY: And I'm Mary. I lead the church's neighborhood outreach.

JONATHAN: Been a while since we saw you for dinner at the shelter, But after seeing your journey in Sunday's paper *(holding a copy),* we just had to pay you a visit.

LENNY: Uh-huh.

MARY: What you said in court.

LENNY: Excuse me?

MARY: What you said . . . forgiving those men who hurt you. I just haven't been able to stop thinking about it. Day and Night. And I just wanted to come and shake your hand.

(She reaches her hand out to Lenny, who hesitates but then takes it.)

You are everything we are asking our congregation to be.

LENNY: Me?

JONATHAN: Why yes.

LENNY: Me?

JONATHAN: The Lord calls us to forgive. To turn the other cheek. As found in Matthew 5:39.

LENNY: Speak up.

JONATHAN: I was quoting Matthew . . . um . . . we'd like to invite you to share your story with our entire church.

LENNY: You serious?

MARY: Yes. We were thinking maybe Wednesday at our mid-week church meeting.

LENNY: The whole church? You're bringing all of them down here?

MARY: Well no, silly. We'd have you come to the church.

LENNY: Uh-huh.

MARY: We would market your appearance over the next few days, so people would know to put the event on their calendars.

JONATHAN: Then we would put a short story about you in a special church bulletin. Here's one we already put together.

(Jonathan hands a program to Lenny.)

LENNY: . . .

JONATHAN: See. We've left spaces for parishioners to take notes . . . about your journey-to-forgiveness.

LENNY: What's this part at the bottom?

JONATHAN: Where?

LENNY: The 'please donate' part?

MARY: That tells the congregation that -- you know -- if they really liked the message they heard, would they please donate to the / church.

JONATHAN: It's just common boilerplate language for a special speaker.

LENNY: Common huh? So when was the last time you "boilered" this?

MARY: Well, we haven't had many speakers lately. Probably a bit more than a year ago / or so.

LENNY: Until me?

MARY: Yes . . . until you. But your story is so / amazing.

LENNY: Then why's the donation part is in the biggest letters?

JONATHAN: Don't get caught up in that Mr. King. Just think through how you might bring your story to life.

MARY: Would likely be, oh, 150-200 people plus maybe a few TV stations there.

JONATHAN: I promise we'll make it as relaxed as we can / for you.

LENNY: Doesn't sound relaxed.

MARY: Oh, It will be. So what can we do to help you prepare?

(Lenny wanders the campsite in deep thought.)

LENNY: So you need me to talk about forgiveness, right?

JONATHAN: Yes.

LENNY: Haven't you already been preaching to them about forgiveness?

JONATHAN: Every Sunday.

LENNY: So why do they need ol Lenny to tell em?

JONATHAN: Cuz you're actually doing it.

LENNY: So you tell em to forgive -- and they know you -- but they don't do it? But you think that I'm gonna show up -- a guy ain't none of 'em ever heard of before Sunday's paper -- and suddenly they're all gonna be reborn or something?

JONATHAN: Well. We'd like to have a spiritual awakening. You / bet.

MARY: Oh yes. Yes, we would. It would be a miracle. Right in front of our / eyes.

LENNY: A miracle? So now I have to deliver a miracle? Me?

JONATHAN: Mr. King.

LENNY: Lenny.

MARY: Lenny. Right now, we have what we call in the church circles as a 'window of opportunity.'

LENNY: A what?

MARY: It's a short period of time where everyone is captivated by something,

JONATHAN: We use that window to deliver a message from the Lord that will stick.

MARY: And right now that window is you.

(Lenny crawls into his tent and then emerges with two dollars.)

LENNY: One for each of you.

(Lenny hands each of them a dollar.)

JONATHAN: Um, Lenny. We don't need this.

LENNY: The donation part in your program says you do.

MARY: Yes, but not your money. We don't need your money.

LENNY: Why not?

JONATHAN: Honestly . . . and I shouldn't say this out of turn . . . but once you speak at the church, you really can write your own ticket.

LENNY: . . .

JONATHAN: As a public speaker.

MARY: Non-profits will pay you, Lenny, to speak in their luncheons and support their fundraisers --

JONATHAN: Just to bring your authentic self to their causes.

(Jonathan puts his dollar back in Lenny's hand.)

MARY: And then you'll have money . . . money that can change your life.

(Mary puts her dollar back in Lenny's other hand.)

LENNY: Change my life? Change my life?

(Lenny defiantly strips off his jacket and shirt down to his bandages. He moves around the campsite as he speaks passionately, causing Mary and Jonathan to back away.)

Have I not changed enough for you when I was on my back -- right there in that spot -- with my hands up protecting me? Trying to shield my eyes from the lighter fluid being dripped down like candle wax? When I could smell the rancid reek of my own flesh burning on my arms right above my face? When I heard those boys laughing like crazy hyenas as I screamed? *(beat)* Is that the change you want your congregational circus to hear about? Why? So they'll donate to this biblical brainstorm you're trying to attach my name to?

(He throws the dollar bills at them.)

My name might be in the paper, But I am not the 'Good News' you're trying to create. I am not the musical montage of your narcissistic narrative. And I am not a king. Deuteronomy 31:6: "Fear not nor be afraid of them for the Lord my God goes with me and will never leave me nor forsake me." You want to tell me about God, then tell me about God, but JESUS CHRIST! *(beat)* Don't. Don't sell my story like you sell your souls . . . if for no other reason than it isn't yours.

JONATHAN: Lenny.

LENNY: Get out. Get out.

MARY: Let us try to say it a different / way.

LENNY: Get out. Get out. Get out. Get out.

(Lenny chases Jonathan and Mary back down the path and away.)

MARY: *(in the distance)* We'll be praying for you.

(Once they're gone, Lenny screams with frustration into his heavy coat to muffle the sound and he puts his shirt and coat back on. He begins to cry softly as he crawls

into his tent to hide.)

SCENE 8

Mark approaches and walks up to the tent's door, talking to Lenny inside.

Hearing Lenny's pain coming from inside, Mark at first considers just letting Lenny be, but he eventually feels compelled to engage with him.

MARK: Don't know that I've heard you sound off like that.

LENNY: Leave me alone.

MARK: What? You too good to be saved now?

LENNY: They didn't want to save me.

MARK: Oh, forgot. You can save yourself.

LENNY: If you're just gonna give me a hard time, take a nap over there quietly or / keep moving.

MARK: Not here to give you a hard time. Just thought you could use some family support.

(Lenny sticks his head out of the tent.)

LENNY: We're family?

MARK: After what we been through? Down here? Yeah. If nothing else, we dress like brothers.

(Both men look at their dirty clothes and laugh together.)

LENNY: Thanks man.

MARK: Getting dark soon. Get some sleep. If you need me, well . . . you know where I'll be.

LENNY: Night, brother Mark.

MARK: Night, brother Lenny.

(Lenny crawls fully back into his tent as Mark exits.)

SCENE 9

As the sun begins going down, Lenny can be heard snoring as a woman approaches carrying a large notepad and a book under her arm.

Deanna, a sociologist, can tell Lenny is asleep, so she starts to look around the campsite, making notes on her notepad. She accidentally kicks one of the buckets, waking Lenny.

LENNY: Mark?

DEANNA: No, Mr. King. It's Deanna Culpepper. Do you have a few minutes to / chat?

LENNY: Who?

DEANNA: I'm Deanna . . . um . . . if you can come out for a moment this would be easier.

(Lenny appears at the tent doorway but doesn't come out.)

There you are. Good evening, Mr. King. Like I said, my name is Deanna Culpepper. I'm a doctor you / see --

LENNY: Already got an appointment at the clinic / on Friday.

DEANNA: Sorry . . . shouldn't have said it that way. I'm a doctor of sociology. I talk to people and learn from their experiences.

LENNY: Hospital send you?

DEANNA: No. They didn't. Your Gazette story popped into the daily digest of my in-box . . . and I thought I'd come find you myself. I have some crackers here if you're hungry.

(Lenny comes out of the tent, takes the crackers and then sits on a bucket. He has a bottle of water and offers a fresh bottle to Deanna.)

Oh, no thank you. Just had some Earl Grey.

LENNY: Earl who?

DEANNA: Just so you know I'm on the up and up, here's a copy of my latest book so you can see my bio. If you're really bored, you can probably read it one night.

(Lenny takes one look and comically throws it in his tent. He moves on to start a fire.)

Ohhh kay. Maybe not. If I can just get five minutes of your time, I just have a few questions.

LENNY: Five minutes?

DEANNA: That ok?

LENNY: K. Sure.

DEANNA: What caused you to be homeless?

LENNY: I have a home.

DEANNA: This tent? This is your home?

LENNY: Uh huh.

DEANNA: Ok . . . what caused you to live in this tent?

LENNY: Why did something have to cause it? Why couldn't I just choose it?

DEANNA: Lenny . . . can I call you Lenny? I'm trying to get you to tell me your life story.

LENNY: Why don't you just ask me that then?

DEANNA: It's an interviewing technique . . . something I learned in Grad School.

LENNY: Asking people what you want is something I learned in kindergarten.

DEANNA: Ok. That I understand.

LENNY: A teacher.

DEANNA: What teacher?

LENNY: Me.

DEANNA: I don't follow.

LENNY: *(eating)* My life story. I was a teacher.

DEANNA: Oh . . . oh. Gotcha.

LENNY: Always liked seeing the lightbulbs go off when my students learned something new.

DEANNA: What did you teach?

(Lenny takes a stick and begins conducting in the air.)

Nice.

LENNY: Music. Instrumental music. School orchestra, marching band, that kind of thing. Watching the inner souls of boys and girls come to life one quarter note at a time.

DEANNA: High school?

(Lenny nods.)

And did you always want to be a teacher?

LENNY: *(stops conducting)* Nah. Wanted to perform. Loved musicals but didn't have the voice. Dreamed of playing my guitar on stage. Wanted to sing and create something new every night.

DEANNA: Ok.

LENNY: Didn't want to get rich. Just be creative.

DEANNA: So what happened?

LENNY: Teaching by day. Auditioning for bands at night. Wasn't great at either. Not like I wanted to be.

DEANNA: Did your family support you? I should say . . . what family did you have in your / life?

LENNY: At first. Yeah. Christine said she wanted me to do what made me happy, but after Tyler was born . . . she was all about 'hey hubby, we got bills to pay' . . . and 'you can't be wasting all our extra money on instruments and amps'.

DEANNA: So, she stopped / supporting you?

LENNY: Didn't want to hear it no more. That pissed me off . . . so I stayed later at the bars trying to find gigs. Drank more. Spent more. Came home one night to a note. Christine said the bank foreclosed . . . and it was my fault . . . and that I had to 'get my priorities together.'

DEANNA: So Christine left you?

LENNY: No. She forgave me. Said she'd give me one last chance to join her and Tyler at her parent's house.

DEANNA: So did you go?

(Lenny shakes his head no.)

Oh, Lenny. What'd you do?

LENNY: Screwed up. Just screwed it all up.

DEANNA: *(beat)* I'm sorry.

LENNY: Saw an ad wanting studio musicians for a big music festival up here. Emptied our savings account and bought a bus ticket from Memphis to Ohio. Thought I'd catch on with a real band and make real money . . . and then I could go back to Christine and Tyler as a hero.

DEANNA: I take it that didn't happen.

LENNY: What? My tent give it away?

DEANNA: Go on Lenny.

LENNY: Should have known the ad was a scam. Damn it. Paid every dollar I had as an entry fee to be one of the 'pool' musicians. They sit in when bands needed a guitarist. But . . . shit.

DEANNA: What'd you do next?

LENNY: Broke. Didn't know anyone here. Couldn't call Christine and say I'd gone to Ohio like a damn fool. Went to the bus stop and tried begging but ended up getting a tooth knocked out and my jacket taken . . . and . . .

DEANNA: And what Lenny?

LENNY: Took my guitar too.

DEANNA: I'm sorry.

LENNY: That was 12 years ago. Haven't seen Christine or my boy . . . or played a single note since.

DEANNA: Whatcha been doing / then?

LENNY: *(shrugs)* Bouncing around the shelters. Got this tent. Came down here about a year ago.

DEANNA: Why here?

LENNY: You know you're the first person to ask me that?

DEANNA: Really?

LENNY: People like to ask why I'm living in a tent. Not why I'm living here.

DEANNA: Well, I ask because I'm curious. Why here? Under the Brown Street Bridge?

LENNY: Shhhh . . .

DEANNA: *(whispering)* I'm curious. Why / here?

LENNY: Not softer. Just shhhhh . . .

(Both go quiet. In the distance, music can be heard over the sounds of the bridge and the wildlife.)

On a clear night I can hear the bands up there playing at the Brown Street Saloon. Lots of songs that I know.

(He closes his eyes and smiles as he listens to the music.)

Don't get that living by a dumpster. I like it.

(He takes a bite.)

DEANNA: Dinner and a show. Nice. Makes you miss home I'll bet.

(Lenny nods yes.)

Anything particular?

LENNY: Dust in the wind.

DEANNA: By Kansas?

LENNY: Always so pretty on acoustic. Reminds me of home. Reminds me of God. So I pitched a tent here, and listened to the music of the night.

DEANNA: *(beat)* Lenny, can I ask you something?

LENNY: . . .

DEANNA: Have you called Christine or Tyler to check on them?

(Lenny shakes his head no.)

LENNY: Wouldn't know what to say. She's moved on I'm sure. He's grown. Mark said he came up here looking for me a few times.

DEANNA: Tyler? You talk to him?

(Lenny shakes his head no.)

LENNY: What am I going to say to him?

DEANNA: How bout 'hello?' See where it goes from / there.

LENNY: Yeah, well that ain't never gonna happen.

DEANNA: But if you / just try.

LENNY: Thanks for the crackers. I think I'd like to have my space back to myself if that's ok.

DEANNA: Sure, Lenny. Mind if I come back sometime? Maybe Friday?

LENNY: If ya want. Guy who wrote this article is coming back that day too.

DEANNA: Gonna speak with him again?

LENNY: Didn't want to the first time. Don't need to again.

DEANNA: So whatcha gonna do? What's next for the King of Brown Street?

LENNY: I ain't no king. God, why can't people get that through their heads?

DEANNA: I'm sorry . . . didn't mean to offend.

LENNY: Starting to think, it's too far gone for me. I mean, look where I am? What has happened to me? I think I'm . . . kind of past it.

DEANNA: Past what?

LENNY: *(softly)* The point of no return.

DEANNA: How so?

LENNY: . . .

DEANNA: Ok . . . I'll let you be.

(Lenny shrugs as if to say 'ok.')

Thank you for . . . well, just thank you. You have a good night, Lenny.

(Deanna exits leaving Lenny in deep thought.)

SCENE 10

Lenny finds a log and to keep the fire going as darkness arrives in full. While warming himself, Lenny starts to shake a bit in sadness.

LENNY: Christine. Oh Christine. God I'm sorry . . . and Tyler. I'm so so sorry.

(A small rock flies from off stage. It misses Lenny but hits his tent. Stunned, he looks around breathing hard until . . .)

PUNK 1: Hey, look whose done taking a shit?

(Punk 1 and Punk 2 emerge.)

PUNK 2: Told you, you couldn't hide forever.
LENNY: Hey . . . leave me alone.

(Punk 1 pushes Lenny off his bucket. Both Punks tower over Lenny next to the fire.)

PUNK 1: Got a present for you, old man. Courtesy of the boys whose lives you ruined.
PUNK 2: You got it coming. Too bad Mark's not here for his ass kicking / too.
LENNY: Leave me alone. Get off me. Get off me. Get off me.

(A shot rings out, and the punks are stunned. They duck down and check to see if they've been shot.)

PUNK 1: What the / hell?

(A gun is heard being cocked.)

PUNK 2: Shit. Go. Go. Go. Go.

(They run off, leaving Lenny still curled up in a ball frightened next to the fire. A figure in a hoody and jeans approaches the fire and goes straight to Lenny.)

LENNY: Please. Please don't hurt me. Leave me alone.

(The figure bends down still holding a handgun and pulls Lenny up to a seated position.)

Leave me alone. Oh God. Please. Please don't hurt me.

(The figure grabs Lenny's wrists to control him before leaning in close. Lenny goes silent and freezes as the man pulls his hood back to expose his face.)

TYLER: Dad. It's me.

Blackout.

Intermission.

SCENE 11

At Rise: Continuous as Tyler has pulled Lenny up to a seated position, and they are face-to-face.

TYLER: Dad. It's me.

LENNY: Wha . . . what . . . what?

TYLER: Dad. It's Tyler. Your son? *(beat)* Here. Let's get you up.

(Tyler pulls Lenny onto a bucket. He then puts his gun in a holster and grabs a bucket to sit on. Lenny sits in disbelief, shivering. Tyler lets out a deep sigh and then takes off his jacket.)

Here. Take it.

(Lenny resists.)

Take it.

(Frustrated, Tyler forces the coat around Lenny to warm him.)

Well . . . nice to see you're still stubborn as a frozen bolt.

LENNY: . . .

TYLER: Well say something, you old fool. You had to have thought this moment might come sooner or later.

LENNY: Hello.

TYLER: That's it? That's all you got to say?

LENNY: Hello . . . Tyler.

TYLER: Well . . . guess I shouldn't have gotten my hopes up.

LENNY: How did you ... what are you doing here?

(Tyler unfolds a copy of the newspaper.)

TYLER: Nice to read you are still alive. And what a lovely throne you get to sit on being that you're a king now. This makes me . . . what? A prince?

(Lenny takes the newspaper Tyler was holding and tosses it in the fire.)

Now what'd you go and do that for? I've read it 10 times.

LENNY: . . .

TYLER: Fine. Guess I'll do the talking. Drove 700 miles to get here. Again.

LENNY: Again?

TYLER: Came just over a year ago. Looked for you at the shelter, but . . . ya know, why am I explaining this? You knew I was there, didn't you?

LENNY: . . .

TYLER: I knew it. I knew it. They took me to your bunk, and suddenly you were gone. Just poof. But I could feel you were there. Avoiding me. Like you were in the mirror staring out or something.

LENNY: Sorry . . .

TYLER: Sorry? Why would you duck me? After all these -- I come all the way from Memphis . . . and you hide from me? Your own son?

LENNY: Didn't know what to say.

TYLER: After all these years, nothing? Nothing to say to the crying boy you swore you were coming back to? You know how long I sat on that porch? Night after night after night?

LENNY: . . .

TYLER: Mom gave up, but I was sure . . . idiot that I am . . . that my father was coming back. My dad just had to play his tunes and then he'd be back. Hell, I even took the acoustic you left behind and learned to play it on the porch. Hoping you'd be impressed when you found out. And as the years went by, I kept strumming along . . . hoping somehow you'd hear it in the distance and . . . *(deep sigh)* . . . just forget it.

LENNY: I . . . I don't know what / to say.

TYLER: So you can say 'I forgive you' to three assholes who torched you, but you can't say anything to your own son?

(Lenny says nothing as he warms at the fire.)

God I'm a fool. The first time I drove here hoping to save you. But this time, I came to make sure you knew the truth.

LENNY: What?

TYLER: You. Left.

(Lenny turns his face away.)

Look at me. You need to hear this. You abandoned me and mom. And no matter what some columnist wrote about your big heart . . . mom and I know the truth. You've got no soul. What you've done can never be forgiven.

(He is moved by watching Lenny struggle to replace a bandage that came off in the tussle. Lenny is using one of the extra bandages the paramedics left.)

Damn it. Here. Let me help you.

(Tyler helps replace the bandage.)

Done.
LENNY: Thanks.
TYLER: Here.

(Tyler reveals cash from his pocket.)

Take it.
LENNY: Don't want it. Don't need / it.
TYLER: Just take it.

(Tyler forces the cash into Lenny's hands.)

Stubborn / son-of-a . . .
LENNY: Thank you.

TYLER: Buy yourself a few meals. I'd leave you my gun too, but God knows what you'd do with it.

LENNY: Thanks.

TYLER: Ya know, get a hotel for a night. Shower up. You'll feel better. How about that?

LENNY: I've got a home here.

TYLER: What? Your tent? Cheap fabric from a Central American sweatshop strapped to some plastic / rods?

LENNY: Don't talk that way about my home.

TYLER: You had a home. *(beat)* You had a home. You blew it. You walked away and . . . *(to himself)* nope . . . not going back there . . . deep breaths, Ty. *(calming himself)* Alright. Here's the deal. I drove up here, so I'm driving back. You need to come home with / me.

LENNY: No.

TYLER: What do you mean no?

LENNY: I mean no. I can't go back. I abandoned . . . I can't go back. I can't.

TYLER: Well you can't stay here.

LENNY: Yes I can. Hey, is that a wedding ring?

TYLER: Stop, just stop. Not doing this now. Look, you stay here below this bridge . . . and your tent's gonna be replaced with a tombstone. Cops tell me that in this part of town, there is a futile flood of crime that claims everything in its path. I'm offering you an ark.

LENNY: But what if?

TYLER: Stop. Just stop.

LENNY: I can't do it.

TYLER: Not gonna argue. 8 a.m. Friday. I'm gonna pull up on top of the bridge. Right up there. Two honks. You'll know it's me. Just leave this -- whatever this site is -- behind and come on up. We'll drive home together. No questions asked.

LENNY: I don't / know.

TYLER: *(frustrated)* Just think about it.

(Tyler stands up to leave.)

My God. Ya know, I actually brought you something.

LENNY: Oh? What?

TYLER: I thought about showing it to you and then breaking it -- right in front of you -- to show you in dramatic detail what you'd done. But looking at you now . . . *(struggles to find the words)* I look at you and I see the blue eyes of the man who taught me chopsticks . . . and played catch in the back yard. But beyond that . . . *(fighting back tears)*

LENNY: What'd you bring?

TYLER: Set it down when I had to pull my gun. It's back there . . . *(gestures under the bridge)* Get it yourself.

LENNY: . . .

TYLER: Friday morning. Two honks. But I swear to God -- if you don't take this life raft, then I'm gone . . . forever.

(Tyler starts to walk away.)

LENNY: Son.

(Tyler stops cold. He turns back around to face Lenny.)

TYLER: What dad?

LENNY: *(mouths)* Thank you.

(Tyler stares for a moment, and then turns around and walks off. Lenny sits in silence at the fire, looks up at the stars and then retreats to his tent to sleep.)

SCENE 12

It's morning as Lenny crawls out of his cold tent. He pulls out a bag of Funyuns for his breakfast. He flips over a bucket, and then starts to softly drum on it.

A woman's voice surprises him.

ALLY: Triplets.

(Lenny stops drumming and looks at the woman.)

You're playing triplets. Three beats played inside a single note-length. Like this.

(She starts to drum on a bucket as Lenny watches.)

Trip-pull-let. Trip-pull-let. Trip-pull-let.

(She stops drumming.)

Typically, there's a number "3" over it on the sheet music. That way the musician knows what the composer meant.

LENNY: You had a good music teacher.

ALLY: I had you.

LENNY: *(beat)* Me?

ALLY: Mr. King. It's Ally Richards. Er, that's my married name. You knew me as Ally --
(together) Henderson.

LENNY: *(together)* Henderson.

ALLY: Oh My God.

LENNY: Henderson. Ally Henderson. You played clarinet, except during marching band season when you played -
(together) the trumpet.

ALLY: *(together)* The trumpet. You have quite the memory.

LENNY: How . . . what . . . what are you doing here?

ALLY: I live here. In Ohio. My wife, Sam, and I moved here after college . . . about 10 years ago, and we have two little girls. I think they're both pretty musical too, but we'll see.

LENNY: But how did you . . .

(Ally holds up a copy of the newspaper.)

ALLY: Felt it was a sign or something. Here I was getting my girls ready for church, and I see you in our local paper. Thought it would be a good / idea.

LENNY: To come see an old teacher?

ALLY: My favorite teacher. *(beat)* Mr. King, I know you've taught hundreds of kids, and I really can't believe you remember me. I can't believe I'm actually seeing / you.

LENNY: Sorry you're seeing me . . . like this.

ALLY: I read your story, and it doesn't surprise me at all.

LENNY: That I live in a tent?

ALLY: That you forgave those young men.

LENNY: But why would you think I would / do that?

ALLY: Mr. King, you were the most caring teacher in school. With everything going on at my home -- not sure if you knew what my father was doing to me. I . . . I guess I'm trying to say that just by being there every day. Saying good morning. Making me -- all of us -- feel like you were genuinely glad to see / us.

LENNY: Ms. Henderson please / stop.

ALLY: You and your music classes made me want to be at school . . . and to learn . . . and to be creative. For some kids it's sports... and for others its acting or academics. For me, it was music. It was you.

LENNY: You're very kind, Ms. Henderson.

ALLY: Let me help you. Please. Even just temporarily. I have an extra room, and you need some place to stay.

LENNY: You say you have two kids?

ALLY: Two girls, yeah.

LENNY: And a wife?

ALLY: Sam. Yes. You would / like her.

LENNY: Then your home is pretty full already.

ALLY: Please Mr. King. Please let me do this for you. I could call some of your other students / too.

LENNY: No. *(beat)* I . . . I really don't think so.

ALLY: But why? Why not let me help / you?

LENNY: I can't.

ALLY: *(beat)* You know that warm feeling you get deep inside when you help someone?

LENNY: Yeah.

ALLY: That feeling that you've done something good for someone? Not because it benefits you, but just because someone needs help . . . and you're there . . . and it's the right thing to do?

LENNY: Yeah.

ALLY: *(forceful)* Why would you deny me that?

LENNY: *(beat)* Ms. Henderson. Means a lot that you're here. What you've / said . . .

ALLY: Why won't you let me help you? *(beat)* Why won't you let me do something for you?

LENNY: I --

ALLY: Why are you being like this? Was I all wrong about you? Did I just romanticize my memories of you as a teacher? Just . . . to make myself feel / better?

LENNY: I was happy to see you. Every day, Ms. Henderson. I was glad to see you and the other students pick up those instruments and make music . . . and find joy just in tapping your toes to the rhythm. My God, it was . . . it was the best part of my day . . . every day . . . for so long . . . teaching you kids was the best part of my life!

ALLY: Yes. / Yes.

LENNY: But I can't accept . . . Ally. I just can't.

(Ally pauses, feeling the wound of Lenny's rejection.)

ALLY: I . . . uh . . . I brought you a sandwich . . . peanut butter . . .

(Ally hands him a sandwich in a Ziplock bag.)

Remembered you liked them . . . and thought . . . uh . . . thought you could use it.

LENNY: That was so . . . *(beat)* Used to tell a story about peanut butter sandwiches at every graduation. Ever heard it?

(Ally shakes her head no.)

Pete and Sally were co-workers when they started dating. They'd have lunch together . . . and every day Pete brought a peanut butter sandwich. Every single day. They fell in love and eventually got married. But then when they'd have lunch together, Pete did something different.

ALLY: What?

LENNY: He cut the crusts off his peanut butter sandwich, And he put them on Sally's plate.

ALLY: Oh.

LENNY: Sally thought this was weird, but she loved Pete with all her heart. So, she said nothing. She just picked up the crusts and ate them. This happened the next day . . . and next week . . . and so on . . . year after year.

ALLY: Ok.

LENNY: Then . . . on their 50th anniversary, Sally just had to have an answer. So she asked, "Peter, love of my life, why do you cut off your crusts and put them on my plate?" And Pete leaned in, and he said . . . because the crusts are my favorite part. And I wanted you to have them.

ALLY: That's so sweet . . . but what's it got / to do with this.

LENNY: Ally, I'm saying that sometimes, from the outside, How a person behaves makes no sense at all. Like giving your crusts to someone else . . . but if you just look closer . . . really look for the small clues, there might be something magical going on.

ALLY: I don't understand why you're choosing to stay here when you could have a bed?

LENNY: I know . . . that you don't. *(beat)* You have no idea what it means that you . . . I miss teaching. I miss students. Students like you, Ally.

(A dejected Ally kisses Lenny on the cheek, and then begins to walk away.)

Make sure you teach those girls of yours about triplets.

(Ally pauses and nods yes, forcing a small smile and then leaves. Lenny painfully watches her go before taking a seat and tapping triplets on the buckets before pausing in deep thought.)

SCENE 13

The voices of Elon and Rita can be heard approaching.

RITA: *(offstage)* Slow down for God's sake.

ELON: *(offstage)* We're almost there. We've got to be –

(Rita and Elon emerge from under the bridge. Rita is walking barefoot carrying her expensive heels.)

RITA: Any farther you're gonna need to call Ricardo to rappel down here and pick me up.

ELON: Well you're the one who . . . *(seeing Lenny)* oh hello. There you are. Good morning.

LENNY: You're gonna hurt yourself.

ELON: Oh, I'm fine.

LENNY: Not you. You. Just stop there. There's glass.

(Lenny places a newspaper over some trash so Rita can walk over it and get closer to the tent.)

RITA: Such a gentleman you are. *(as she walks on the newspaper)*

LENNY: Enough blood already spilled down here. Don't need your feet getting cut and adding to the pool.

RITA: Oh, forgive my bare piggies . . . but some things just must be preserved. These are Christian Louboutins.

LENNY: So you're a Christian?

RITA: Not Christian as in . . . ya know, never mind. Hello. Hi. You're the Mister King?

ELON: *(to Rita)* Who else would he be? *(to Lenny)* Elon Goodweather. Elon is fine. Thanks for allowing Miss Turner --

RITA: Rita.

ELON: Rita . . . and I . . . would like to have a moment of your time.

LENNY: Whachoo want?

(Rita snaps a copy of the newspaper to Elon, who puts his arm around Lenny like a salesman.)

ELON: What would you say if I told you that Sunday's front page story was just the beginning of your legacy. A future not of Lenny King the homeless man *(majestic)* but of Lenny King, Community Ambassador?

LENNY: What's that?

ELON: You've become a name, my friend.

RITA: A face.

ELON: A living, breathing, talking icon of what Akron is all about.

LENNY: You the mayor?

ELON: Oh . . . God no. Couldn't survive on that salary.

RITA: We're deal makers. We see neighborhoods that need . . . shall we say . . . a makeover. And then we find the right investors to lift those neighborhoods up.

ELON: Reborn to a new life with new amenities and a whole new future.

RITA: That's where you come in, Mr. King.

LENNY: Doing what?

RITA: Being the face of change. Of progress. Of . . . the story yet to be written.

ELON: *(to Rita)* Oh that's good.

RITA: *(to Elon)* Right?

LENNY: I don't write stories.

RITA: We'll do the writing. It's like this. You know where the Northside Suites are?

ELON: We built those.

RITA: We take you there . . . get you a suite . . . some new clothes . . . a haircut.

ELON: Definitely.

RITA: And then you sit with Sydney, our PR girl.

ELON: Love her.

RITA: And she works with you to . . . refine . . . your story. The journey that brought you to our fair town . . . where your character and integrity led you to rise up . . . and become the hero we didn't know we needed.

ELON: Think about it. *(visualizing a billboard)* Find your true self here . . . at King's Corners. Sounds amazing, right? Right?

LENNY: King's Corners?

(Lenny suddenly notices Mark has appeared under the bridge and is observing the conversation.)

RITA: You're the king. This is your kingdom. Your story *(holding newspaper)* makes people want to live here. Right here.

LENNY: Under my bridge?

RITA: God you're precious. No. In the town homes we're going to build right above here. King's Corners.

(Rita flamboyantly hands Lenny a development brochure.)

Right Along Brown Street.

ELON: Look, people want two things for their futures. Hope and Transformation.

RITA: And the Lenny King story of forgiveness brings both.

ELON: And you did it . . . right here . . . from under this bridge.

RITA: An epic adventure worth sharing with the world!

ELON: We'll even give you an apartment to call your own.

LENNY: Can Mark come too?

(Mark laughs at this.)

ELON: *(ignoring Lenny's question)* . . . and again it's all here at . . . drum roll please.

(Rita makes a drumroll sound.)

King's Corners.

LENNY: King's Corners?

ELON: God, it's like the baseball field in the corn. All ya gotta do Lenny . . . all it takes from you . . . is just to say yes!

(Lenny moves away from the couple to gather his thoughts. Lenny stares at Mark who leans against the bridge walls and responds by shrugging his shoulders as if to say "It's up to you, Lenny.")

LENNY: I ain't no king.

RITA: Ah, excuse me?

LENNY: I ain't no king.

ELON: I don't think you're hearing this / right.

LENNY: And I don't think you're hearing me.

RITA: You're seriously gonna turn this down? To do what? Keep living here in this rats / nest?

LENNY: I beg your pardon, lady?

ELON: Rita. I got this. *(to Lenny)* My friend, we're gonna give you some time to think on this.

RITA: You get an apartment . . . a monthly stipend . . .

ELON: And a chance for the world to embrace your forgiveness story forever. *(beat)* You've got til Friday morning to say yes.

LENNY: Or what?

RITA: Or we and our investors find the next Akron also-ran who actually does want to succeed. Trust me, we won't have to look hard.

ELON: And then . . . we evict you. Move you on to a new bridge you can hide under. *(beat)* Friday, Lenny.

(Elon and Rita exit with smug attitudes walking right past Mark.)

SCENE 14

Mark makes faces at Elon and Rita. He swipes his hands like he's raining money but they don't react.

MARK: Did the hospital shift your polar alignment or something?

LENNY: Hell if I know.

MARK: Cuz for a guy who used to repel everyone . . . you sure are a magnet of masculinity now.

LENNY: Can you believe those people?

MARK: Believe it brother. Money and a suite to live in? You got more options now than a wall street broker.

LENNY: Quit.

MARK: A photo book, a bed at the shelter, on tour with the church . . . the subject of a research study . . . old students seeking you out . . . and now a development based on your life story? Oh . . . and let's not forget Tyler came / calling.

LENNY: And all I had to do was forgive somebody.

MARK: You didn't just forgive somebody. You forgave three killers in / waiting.

LENNY: Stop.

MARK: You know I'm right.

LENNY: I said stop.

MARK: Damn it, Lenny.

LENNY: They had futures.

MARK: No they didn't. If they hadn't hurt you, they were bound to hurt or kill someone else.

LENNY: *(loud and passionate)* That's not who they are. Those kids could have made something of themselves.

MARK: Always believing in the good in people.

LENNY: Well someone should --

MARK: *(louder than Lenny)* Just because they didn't kill you . . . didn't keep them from killing that night . . . did it?

LENNY: *(beat)* I tried, Mark. I tried to get you.

MARK: It's ok --

LENNY: I was crawling towards you.

MARK: I know --

LENNY: I didn't know they had that gun. I didn't know.

MARK: It's ok --

LENNY: It was so loud. My ears were ringing when they left you and started pouring the lighter fluid. Oh, God.

MARK: I know Lenny. I know. Deep breaths.

LENNY: You should be here. Brother, you should still be here.

MARK: Yeah, I should. But you did what I couldn't. You did what all these bogus intellectual imposters traipsing through here only wish they had the courage to rise up and accomplish. Lenny, you looked pure evil in the face -- stared into the demon eyes that killed me right over there . . . locked eyes with those who cackled as they scarred your body for life -- and you said, 'you don't get to rob me of another moment. Your actions don't get to own my life just because you failed to take it.'

LENNY: And for what?

MARK: Lenny. Lenny??? You forgave them. Not just for them. For you too. And now every moment for the rest of your life isn't an endless trap of being a victim. Do you know how many people are stuck in that maze of mayhem? Weighing them down . . . consuming their every thought . . . day after day . . . reliving being a victim? But you rid yourself of that weight because you never put it on your back . . . and that, my friend, means you got options. Not just what these newcomers are offering unless that's what you want. But you got choices, man. And you don't have to provide an explanation for it. You don't owe anyone anything . . . except yourself.

LENNY: You really believe that?

MARK: You forgave those kids. Now it's time you forgave yourself, Lenny. Time to stop avoiding mirrors cuz you can't look yourself in the eyes. Time you realized you are worthy of love and respect. And it's time for you to do for yourself, what you said Jesus led you to do with them boys.

LENNY: I can't. I just can't / Mark.

MARK: You survived being set on fire. There is nothing you can't do.

LENNY: What about Tyler?

MARK: That's on you.

LENNY: Seriously, what do I do?

MARK: Make a decision and don't look back. Be a rhinoceros. *(becomes animated)*

LENNY: *(laughing)* A rhinoceros? You serious?

MARK: Follow me here. *(animated)* Focus that big horn on your target and just charge right at it. Make money here or go back with Tyler. Write the musical you always talked about. Or better yet, teach again. But it's time to let yourself out of this tent -- this personal prison where you lay your head under this bridge -- and live. It's time to live, Lenny.

(After a few moments of silence, a bright light swells from under the bridge.)

LENNY: No.

MARK: . . .

LENNY: C'mon Mark.

MARK: It's time. I'm nothing but a houseguest at this point.

LENNY: No.

MARK: Don't want to wear out my welcome.

LENNY: That could never happen.

MARK: I hear heaven has some primo mattresses. *(chuckles)* It's time. *(beat)* It's my time to go. And it's your time to forgive yourself . . . and move on.

(Mark walks toward the light, but then stops and takes one last look at Lenny.)

LENNY: I never felt alone down here as long as you were nearby.

(Mark responds by making a horn on his head like the rhinoceros. He smiles, and then turns and walks away confidently into the light.)

SCENE 15

Lenny waits for a moment and then walks towards the light where Mark left, but as he gets close, the light disappears.

As Lenny turns to walk back to his tent, he trips on something in the grass. It's the item that Tyler brought him. It's an acoustic guitar in a case. It's Lenny's old guitar that Tyler learned to play. Lenny is speechless as he picks up the case, takes it to his tent, and then takes out the guitar.

Sitting next to the fire, Lenny tunes it for a moment and reacts with a joy he hasn't felt in decades. He plays a chord or two. Pauses. And then begins playing the opening chords to "Dust in the Wind".

Note: He sings the first short verse only.

LENNY: *(singing)* "I close my eyes. Only for a moment and the moment's gone. All my dreams, pass before my eyes, a curiosity. Dust in the wind."

(He stops playing guitar as light snow begins to fall and he's illuminated by the full moon. Taking in the moment, he delivers the next line in a whisper.)

All we are is Dust in the Wind.

(He puts the guitar in the case. He puts out the evening fire and smiles. As he heads to the tent, he seems to survey his surroundings for the last time. He's made up his mind about what's next. Lenny crawls inside the tent.)

SCENE 16

Friday morning. Sunrise illuminates the area.
  Bob arrives and begins looking around the site.

BOB: Mr. King? Good morning. Mr. King? *(to himself)* Where'd he get off to? *(louder)* Lenny? You here / Lenny?

(Collin appears.)

COLLIN: Are you looking for Lenny King?

BOB: I am. I think he must be sleeping in there. How do you know him?

COLLIN: We have some legal matters to discuss. And you?

BOB: Well, we made contact through the / newspaper.

(Mary saunters in riding the joy of the Lord.)

MARY: A beautiful morning to visit my . . . oh, excuse me. I didn't realize there was a Friday revival down here.

COLLIN: It's not. And you are?

MARY: That's my business, but needless to say, I'm here to continue to bless Mr. King's relationship with the Lord. That is if he is coming out. *(to the tent)* Lenny. Good morning. It's Mary. Hoping maybe we could pray / together.

ELON: *(joining the group)* Excuse me folks, if you're here to look at this property, you're too late.

BOB: I'm sorry?

ELON: My firm is acquiring more than ten acres, including

this space under the bridge. And we're ready to form a formal partnership with Mr. / King.

COLLIN: Partnership? Um, Lenny should really have an attorney look / that over.

(They all begin talking over one another, arguing about how they have the right to talk to Lenny first.

After a few moments, Deanna arrives, observes, and then interrupts the group.)

DEANNA: Will you listen to yourselves?

(The group stops talking and stares at Deanna.)

ELON: And who the hell do you think you are?

MARY: *(to Elon)* Watch your language.

ELON: You don't get to talk to me like that.

DEANNA: I'm studying Mr. King, and I won't have you all messing up this unique research I've / started.

BOB: Look, all of you. I wrote this story. I found Lenny and his famed tale of forgiveness. None of you would even know he's here without my article. *(holds up a copy of the paper)* So I'm going first. End of story.

(All continue bickering over one another.)

Lenny come out here.

(No response.)

Lenny, I know we were all way too loud but please . . .

can you just come out here . . . and we can just chat about the week you've had and the days ahead?

(No response.)

COLLIN: See, you've all overwhelmed him. This is madness. Lenny?

(Collin moves to the side of the tent next to Bob, and Elon, Mary and Deanna follow suit as they all talk at once trying to coax Lenny out of the tent to their point of view.

As the mob begins shaking the tent, Deanna raises her voice and stops the group from speaking.)

DEANNA: Quiet! All of you! Quiet! *(to the tent)* Lenny, just tell us what you want to do!

(Dead silence as everyone leans into the tent.

Two honks are heard overhead. The group look at one another not knowing what to make of it. Bob and Collin put their hands on the front of the tent and pull open the door, and the entire tent collapses. Lenny has vanished.)

COLLIN: What the hell?

(All respond with disbelief.)

MARY: Where is he? Where's Lenny?

(Bob reaches into the flat fabric that used to be a tent

and pulls out a copy of the newspaper. The word "King" has been crossed off with marker and replaced with "Baron." He holds it high for everyone to read: The Baron of Brown Street.

A clear sound is heard from above of a car pulling away.)

BOB: Well thanks everyone for chasing away the King of Brown / Street.

COLLIN: Um, *(pointing at the newspaper)* I don't think that's accurate anymore.

ELON: You might want to hire him for your / newsroom.

BOB: I blame all of you for this.

MARY: *(to Collin)* You especially.

COLLIN: Fine. Sue us. You think you scare / me?

ELON: What a colossal waste of / time.

COLLIN: Oh, shut up.

ELON: This is on you. And you.

DEANNA: You have any idea what this will / cost me? To find a new research subject?

MARY: The Lord will not forget what you all have done here today.

(They all loudly blame one another (ad-libs) as they walk away frustrated that Lenny is gone.

The scene is now empty and quiet except for sounds of the bridge overhead. The familiar sound of deer in the woods is heard once again. The quiet is broken when Lenny crawls out from under the burned-out mattress where he'd somehow hidden himself by escaping unseen from the back of the tent. He checks to make sure everyone is gone, and then stands up, smiles and looks to the deer.)

LENNY: Well, hello there. I know you.

(Lenny smiles, picks up the acoustic guitar case, and then walks under the bridge and out of sight.)

Blackout.

END OF PLAY

GATHER BY THE GHOST LIGHT

ORIGINAL STORIES FOR RADIO THEATER

GATHER BY THE GHOST LIGHT is a storytelling podcast in radio theater format. Think of the Ghost Light as your campfire. Gather around and listen to stories from a variety of genres. Playwright Jonathan Cook and Devon McSherry are the hosts of the series and most of the stories you hear were originally written as short stage plays and they now have been adapted to audio plays with professional voice actors and immersive sound effects. The audio plays produced on this podcast give these talented playwrights an even wider audience for their stories. We welcome you to join us in this journey as we extend the voices of emerging playwrights!

Available wherever you get your podcasts!
For more information, please visit:
www.gatherbytheghostlight.com

Gather by the Ghost Light annual anthologies of audio plays are all available through Ghost Light Publications!

BETWEEN DOG AND WOLF

by Cris Eli Blak

2M, 1W, DRAMA

WINNER OF THE 2024 CHARLES M. GRETCHELL NEW PLAY AWARD
High school friends Blake, Patrick, and Mara reunite at a hotel the day before their 10-year reunion. Forever traumatized by the school shooting that took place their junior year, the three try and fail to relive painful memories and heal broken friendships.

BOBBY IS DEAD

by Marty Matfess

2M, 3W, COMEDY

Chris has been madly in love with his best friend Annie for years, but she's only been interested in dating everyone else but him. After Annie's recent break up with her boyfriend Bobby, Chris feels this may finally be what he needs to find his way into her heart, but just like that ... she's already moved on to another guy she met at a coffee shop. Being the good friend that he is, Chris has agreed to hang out with the new guy's visiting sister while they go out on a date. Oh, and let's not forget about Bobby. Turns out he's not taking the break up too well and Chris is now caught between an aggressive ex-boyfriend while having to keep new guy's sister company. A play about love, lust, and getting shot in the head.

IN THE SLUSH
by Daniel Prillaman

2M, 2W, HORROR

2023 FINALIST FOR NEW DRAMATISTS' PRINCESS GRACE AWARD

Newlywed Laura Beth Gardner has it all. A loving husband, a baby on the way, and a usually delightful job. But this weekend, tasked with reading through her publishing house's slush pile, she encounters a mysterious manuscript that claims she isn't human. That her husband isn't who he says he is. And that she's a vessel for her unborn child, who is actually the Second Coming of an ancient darkness that will devour the world. It has to be some sort of joke.

…But what if it's not?

A cosmic horror about identity, creation, and the things we'll do to realize our dreams.

THE DESTINATION
by Ryan Kaminski

2M, 3W, HORROR

In the midst of a blizzard, a group of strangers seek refuge in a secluded motel, unaware that the motel proprietor and a mysterious stranger will make them part of a deadly game. A psychological horror play set during the holiday season.

KINGDUMB

by Jonathan Cook

10M, 6W, COMEDY

There's a new King in the land that has initiated a mysterious new tax on the citizens. Outraged, the region's finest Clock fixer, aka "Time Repair Specialist", recruits some of the most unlikely rebels to help him develop a plan to overthrow the King. Their plotting takes them on a comedic journey through perilous mountain tops all the way to the palace itself where they confront this vile King face to face. Kingdumb is a medieval fantasy comedy full of absurdist humor and illogical behavior.

ALL BARK, NO BITE

by Kara Emily Krantz

2M, 3W, COMEDY

Charlotte and Eugene live a quiet, no-nonsense lifestyle surrounded by sudoku and argyle. Robert and Bella are boisterous and messy and ridiculously in love. Then there's the neighbor, Suzanne, who basically doesn't know what's going on, but definitely has something to say about it. Sure, relationships can be exciting! They can also be confusing, unexpected, and expose us to profound emotional risk. However, relationships are almost always worth exploring, and if we're willing to be vulnerable, can fill up the empty or wounded spaces in our hearts. And if that doesn't work? Well, get a dog.

www.ingramcontent.com/pod-product-compliance
Lightning Source LLC
Chambersburg PA
CBHW070426310726

48977CB00003B/856